God is Good

God Makes

Seeds

That

Grow

By Mrs. James Swartzentruber

Pictures by Daniel Zook and Lester Miller

To the Teacher:

This book is designed to give constructive reading practice to pupils using the grade one *Bible Nurture and Reader Series.* It uses words that have been introduced in the reader or can be mastered with phonics skills taught by Unit 3, Lesson 10. A few new words also appear in the story, printed in italics. At the end of the book, these words are listed with pronunciations and / or illustrations to help the children to learn them on their own. Be sure the children understand that the words are vocabulary or sound words except the words in italics, and where to look to learn the new words if they need help. They should be able to read this book independently.

Books in this series with their placement according to reading and phonics lessons:

Printed in U.S.A.

ISBN 978-07399-0059-8

Catalog no. 2251

Chop, chop. Mother's hoe made a hole in the ground. Joy dropped one, two, three corn seeds into the hole. David covered the seeds with dirt.

"I wish we could eat fresh sweet corn right now," said David.

"Oh, sweet corn is good!" said Joy. "But we will have to wait a long time to get corn from these seeds."

"Yes, it will take a long time," said Mother. "We will need to hoe the plants so that they grow faster. Corn cannot grow very well if there are too many weeds close to it."

"Mother, how can little seeds like these grow to be such big plants?" asked David. "This is such a little seed, but a corn plant is big. It has lots of corn on it, too. And it is all from one little seed!"

"God makes it grow," said Mother. "We cannot make seeds grow. We can put them into the ground.

"God sends the rain . . . and

makes the sun shine . . . That

helps sweet corn seeds to grow into big plants. Then we have more sweet corn. He makes the bean plants grow big, too. Then we have more beans."

"We get beans from bean seeds," said David.

"And peas from pea seeds," said Joy.

Mother came to the end of the
row. "We are done now, and here
comes Father home from town."

David and Joy helped Mother
take the seeds into the house.
Then they ran out to Father.

"We planted sweet corn!" said David.

"And peas and beans and many other things," said Joy.

"Good," said Father. "Now

when it rains, they can start to grow. I have something for you to take into the house."

Father gave a bag to David. He gave one to Joy, too. "I will take the big bag," he said.

"We can eat right away," said Mother when they came into the house.

Father, Mother, David, Joy,

and little May sat down to eat.

When they were finished, Father said, "David, I have something for you and Joy. It is in the bag that I gave you to

bring in. Will you please find it and bring it to me?''

David took some things out of the bag. Then he saw something he and Joy liked very much. It looked like corn, but it was *candy*.

David gave the bag of corn *candy* to Father. Father opened

it and gave some to David and some to Joy.

David did not eat his *candy* very fast. He wanted to keep it a long time. He ate some.

David held the *candy* in his hand. It was so good. He wished he could have some every day.

David looked at the *candy*. He was thinking about something. He was thinking about planting sweet corn and beans. One little seed would grow into a big plant and give much more. Why not plant one of these, too? It looked like corn. If it would grow, then he and Joy could eat much more corn *candy*!

"I will try it," David said to himself. He made a hole in the soft dirt. He planted the corn *candy* just like the other seeds.

Every day David looked to see if the corn *candy* was growing. There were little green plants where they had planted the beans and peas. Soon there were little plants where they had planted the sweet corn, too. But

David could not see anything where he had planted the corn *candy*.

David put water on the ground where he had planted the corn *candy*. Still it did not grow. He waited many days, but there was no little green plant where he

had planted the *candy* corn.

"I cannot see why my corn *candy* does not grow," he was thinking one day. "I will see if it is still there."

David dug down with his *fingers*. There it was. But it did

not look good to eat. It had dirt on it, and it was full of holes. Something had been eating it.

Mother came to see what David was looking at. She saw the corn *candy*.

"It does not grow," said David looking at Mother. "Why not? I planted it a long time *ago*. I put water on it, too."

Mother smiled. "*Candy* does not grow because God did not make it," she said. "It looks like corn, but it is not corn. No one but God can make seeds that grow. People can make things that look like seeds, but they cannot make them grow."

Mother went back to her work. David looked at the corn *candy* for a long time while he was thinking.

"God can make things that grow. People cannot do that. God does many good things. He makes the seeds grow. He makes the big trees. He makes rain and snow. He makes the sun to shine in the daytime and the moon and stars to shine at night. God made everything very good. He is a good God."

candy (can·dē)

fingers (fing·gėrz)

ago (a·gō)